One summer day in Green Meadow, the Get Along Gang was drinking lemonade in Hoofnagel's Ice Cream Emporium. Montgomery Moose, the gang's leader, stood up. "Boy, it's hot today. Let's go swimming." Everyone agreed that was a terrific idea.

1

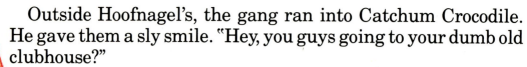

Outside Hoofnagel's, the gang ran into Catchum Crocodile. He gave them a sly smile. "Hey, you guys going to your dumb old clubhouse?"

Rocco Rabbit, the toughest member of the gang, faced Catchum. "Yeah. What's it to you?" The wily crocodile didn't answer. He just chuckled and walked away.

Rocco frowned. "I don't like this. Catchum looked too happy, and that usually means trouble."

But the gang forgot about Catchum as they hurried to their clubhouse. The clubhouse was a little red caboose that stood on abandoned tracks at the edge of town.

3

But when the gang reached the spot where the caboose should have been, it was nowhere to be seen. In its place was a note to Bingo from Catchum.

Bingo read the note aloud.

Dear Bingo "Bet-It-All" Beaver,
You lost the bet.
I won--so I get the potbellied stove.
The stove was inside the caboose, so I took the caboose.
Catchum C.

Little Portia Porcupine
began to cry. "Oh, Bingo, why
did you make a bet with
Catchum? Now we've lost
the clubhouse."

Bingo felt
miserable. "I'm sorry,
Portia. I'll go tell
Catchum that he
can't have the
clubhouse. I only bet
him the stove."

5

Woolma Lamb fussed with her curls. "That crude crocodile. My comb and brush were in the clubhouse, and I look a fright. What were Bingo and Catchum betting about anyway?"

Rocco puffed out his chest. "That doesn't matter. What matters is getting the clubhouse back, and I'm the one to do it."

"No, I think we should have Officer Growler arrest Catchum!" Montgomery spoke up. "Hold it, everyone. We need a plan."

6

The gang sat down to listen to Montgomery. "Catchum probably had the swamp rats pull our caboose onto the tracks in Gummyfoot Swamp, so that's where we're going."
Bingo spoke up sadly. "There are miles of track in the swamp. I bet we'll never find it."
"I bet we will, if we stick together."

Montgomery sent Bernice Bear off to find Dotty Dog. And he asked Rocco to find a rope and some whistles. "If anyone gets lost, they can whistle for help."

At the same time, deep in Gummyfoot, Catchum and the swamp rats had rolled the little red caboose to the edge of the Big Bog. The Big Bog was the biggest, deepest mudhole in the swamp.

GREEN MEADOW

MAIN TRACK

BIG
ROCK

THE
GET ALONG
GANG

MAIN TRACK

LELAND'S LAIR →

CATCHUM'S HIDEAWAY

SNAKE PLACE

GLOOMY GLEN

GUMMYFOOT SWAMP

TERRIBLE TREE

SWAMP RATS

CLUBHOUSE CABOOSE

CLUBHOUSE CABOOSE

CATCHUM CROCODILE

LELAND LIZARD

BIG BOG

9

Soon the rats were busy hiding the caboose with plants and vines. Catchum leaned out of the caboose and examined their work. "More vines, more slime! More camouflage for my new hideaway. If the Get Along Gang ever gets this far, I want them to walk right by without seeing it."

Inside the caboose, Catchum paced nervously. He poked a finger at his friend, Leland Lizard. "Are you sure you checked along the tracks leading to here? I don't want any clues for our Get Along Gang friends to find when they come looking for the caboose."

"Sure, Boss, I checked. They'll never find us."

Meanwhile, the Get Along Gang walked down the tracks into the swamp. Soon they came to a place where the tracks split in two. Which was the right way?

Braker Turtle walked up and down each track slowly. "The weeds on the tracks to the right are all squashed and bent. I'd say our clubhouse went that way." The gang followed him.

Before long they came to another place where the tracks split in two. Braker scratched his head. "The caboose couldn't have rolled to the right. There's a big rock there. We should go to the left."

Just then, Woolma spotted something. "Look, next to the rock! There's one of my new hair ribbons. It must have fallen out when the caboose went by. I think the rats put the rock here to trick us. Let's go down these tracks."

"Woolma's right. Let's go this way, gang." Montgomery led them around the rock and down the track, on toward the Big Bog.

Finally the gang came around the last bend before the Big Bog. They saw the caboose dead ahead. Bingo gave an excited shout. "Hey! That's ours, Catchum! Give it back!" The gang raced down the tracks toward their beloved clubhouse.

The swamp rats saw the Get Along Gang charging toward them and began to scurry away. But Catchum jumped out of the caboose and yelled at them. "Stop, you ratty rodents! Grab hold and pull this red hunk of junk off the track and into the bog. It's *partly* mine, and if I can't have it, no one can."

Montgomery ran to one end of the caboose and tied on the rope he'd been carrying. "Okay, everybody, grab hold and *pull!*" The rats grabbed the other end of the caboose and pulled in the opposite direction.

It was a tug of war. The gang was strong, but the rats were stronger. The caboose inched toward the bog.

Montgomery saw they were losing the battle. He grabbed his whistle. "Quick everyone, blow your whistles! Maybe Dotty and Bernice will hear us."

The gang blew their whistles as loudly as they could, but no one came. Catchum called from the other end of the caboose. "Sorry, Montgomery, but it's no help to whistle while you work."

Suddenly Dotty Dog, Bernice, and Officer Growler appeared. The caboose teetered at the end of the tracks as Dotty and the others grabbed the rope. "Hold on, gang! We're here now! When I say pull, *really* pull. All together now. One, two, three—PULL!"

21

The gang pulled with all its might. Suddenly the caboose jerked to a halt. The swamp rats lost their grip and fell backward into the bog.

Officer Growler took charge of the rest. He rounded up Catchum, Leland, and the dripping rats. "I'll keep my eye on them until tomorrow. Then they'll put your clubhouse back where it belongs and clean it up. But I'm afraid you'll still have to give Catchum the potbellied stove."

GREEN MEADOW

The next day the caboose was back and Dotty was busy designing a new stove for the clubhouse. Montgomery walked over to Bingo. "By the way, what was the bet you made with Catchum?"

Bingo blushed. "I bet him that I could find his hideaway in the swamp. But I couldn't, not by myself. But when the whole gang stuck together, we found it double-quick. After all, sticking together is what the Get Along Gang does best!"